Dear Reader—

When I was growing up, my mother, my father, my sister, and I celebrated the holidays at my grandmother's house along with my aunts, uncles, cousins, nieces, and nephews. We also celebrated the holidays with our extended family—our friends and neighbors—by going door to door and visiting each other's houses. I thought a lot about those childhood memories while I was writing this book and realized that my own personal definition of "family"—all the people in your life you love and care for—was formed all those many years ago.

So, I wish you and everyone you share your holidays with all the best.

—Joe

For Haddi, Sallie, and Livy,
the newest branches on our family tree.
—Uncle Joe

ISBN 978-0-545-51745-4

12 11 10 9 8 7 6 5 4 3 2 1   12 13 14 15 16 17/0

Printed in Singapore   46

First Scholastic printing, November 2012

www.holidayhillfarm.com

Spookley
the Square Pumpkin™
A FAMILY TO BE THANKFUL FOR

Written and created by Joe Troiano

illustrated by Mary O'Keefe Young

A HOLIDAY HILL FARM® BOOK

SCHOLASTIC INC.

Halloween had come and gone,
it was time for Thanksgiving
on Holiday Hill Farm.

Spookley wondered about this new holiday.
Did you get treats, and wear costumes,
and give candy away?

Jack Scarecrow said, "No.
It's not like that at all.
Thanksgiving's *another* holiday
that comes every fall.

"It's a day when families gather together
and give thanks for having each other forever."

Spookley thought about Thanksgiving,
and felt a little sad.
Everyone gathered around
to see why he felt bad.

"I don't have a family," Spookley said with a moan.
"I'm the only square pumpkin that has ever grown.

"I know it is Thanksgiving,
but I'm not really sure
a square pumpkin has something
to be thankful for."

Jack said, "Spookley, my friend,
maybe you should think a bit more."

Spookley thought and thought as he shuffled along.
He thought, *I wish I had a family and a place I belong.*

Spookley was shuffling
down the first garden row
when a pod full of peas shouted,
"Spookley, don't go!

"Spend Thanksgiving with us
and you'll have lots of fun.
You may not be a pea,
but we'll treat you like one."

"Maybe later," Spookley said.
Then he turned and once more
shuffled off to find something
to be thankful for.

And in the next row . . .

The tomatoes said, "Howdy."
The corn called, "Yoo-hoo!"
The carrots said,
"Stay, Spookley, stay and we'll play with you.

"Spend Thanksgiving with us
and you'll have lots of fun.
You may not be a carrot,
but we'll treat you like one."

"Not now," Spookley said.
Then he turned and once more
shuffled off to find something
to be thankful for.

And in the next row . . .

The squash called, "Good morning."
The peppers said, "Hi."
The beans said,
"Why, Spookley, why are you passing us by?

"Spend Thanksgiving with us
and you'll have lots of fun.
You may not be a bean,
but we'll treat you like one."

"Can't stay," Spookley said.
Then he turned and once more
shuffled off to find something
to be thankful for.

And in the next row . . .

The eggplants said, "Slow down."
The onions said, "Whoa!"
The potatoes said,
"Stop! Spookley, stop!
That's as far as you should go."

And in the next row . . .
well . . . there was no next row!

Spookley had shuffled too far.
He was lost and alone.
He wondered why he wandered
so far from his home.

Now he wished he had stayed
with his friends and played.
Instead, he was alone—
alone and afraid.

He called out for help
and hoped in his heart
that someone would hear him.
Someone did . . .
and that was just the start.

The potatoes heard Spookley
and knew something was wrong.
So they told the onions
who passed it along.

The onions told the eggplants,
who let the beans know
so they could tell the peppers
growing in the next row.

Then the peppers told the squash,
who let the carrots know
so they could tell the corn
growing in the next row.

Then the corn told the tomatoes,
who let the peas know
so they could tell Jack . . .

standing in the next row.

And when Jack heard the news, he came running on the double.
So did all Spookley's friends once they heard there was trouble.

Spookley saw them all coming
and was thankful as could be.
And they hugged him,
and hugged him,
and hugged him times three.

Spookley smiled at them sweetly,
and could finally see
they were more than just friends—
they were his family.

And that's what Spookley really had to discover—
that no one family tree
grows quite the same as another.

And that's why Thanksgiving is such a special day.
It's a chance for people who love you to say—

My *life is much better*
because you *are here,*
and that a family is something to be thankful for
each and every day of the year.

Spookley thought about Thanksgiving,
and all he had seen,
and decided it was his favorite holiday.

Well . . . right after Halloween!